PLATINUM TEEN SERIES

A Division of Preciousstymes Entertainment

INTRODUCES...

DYMOND

IN

THE ROUGH

By

Precious

Note: Sale of this book without a front cover may be unauthorized. If this book is purchased without a cover, it may have been reported to the publisher as "unsold or destroyed". Neither the author nor the publisher may have received payment for the sale of this book.

This novella is a work of fiction. Any resemblance to real people, living or dead, actual events, establishments, is intended to give the fiction a sense of reality and authenticity. Other names, characters, places, and incidents are either products of the author's imagination or are used fictitiously.

Precioustymes Entertainment
229 Governors Place, #138
Bear, DE 19701
precious@platinumteen.org
www.platinumteen.org
www.myspace.com/platinumteenmovement

Library of Congress Control Number: 2004098611
ISBN# 0-9729325-2-6
Cover Design: www.ccwebdev.com
Back cover model: Mikeira Moore
Editors: Joanie Smith & Jahmya Ross

Copyright © 2004 by Precioustymes Entertainment. ALL RIGHTS RESERVED, including the right to reproduce this book or portions thereof in any form whatsoever without the permission from the publisher, except by reviewer(s) who may quote a brief passage(s) to be printed in a newspaper, magazine, radio interview, documentary.

First Trade Paperback Edition Printing April 2005 - Printed in Canada

Dedications

This book is dedicated to my Diamonds in the rough…

Jahmya, Mecca, Jasmine, Keyontia, Mikeira, Ki-Ki, Sabrina, Starr, Jade, Robynn, Jayvonna, Brittany, Alexis, Martina, Tish, Carltilia, Mira, Honey, Emerald, Shawnai, Tracion, Alina, Miesha, Candice, Alisha, Rebecca, Jakeia, Lanae, Keondra, Maisha, Ira, Charnay, Jasminc, Tawana, Marshay, Diamond, Ronequa, Dominique

I thank God that he placed you in my life… even if it were for a season.

A special dedication to Jahmya Ross for helping make this project a success!

Intro

Don't you just love my picture on the back of the book when I was four years old? Wasn't I quite the cutest little girl you've ever seen? That's me, "Dymond in the Rough." Check me out now though on the front cover at 14 years old.

I'm ten times cuter right?... shined up and bling-blingin'. Don't think I'm being vain. I'm just confident of myself.

My name is Dymond. Not a ruby, not a sapphire, not an emerald - but the top of the line... a diamond. I'm an only child from a single parent household. My mom's name is Melody and she definitely holds the fort down. My father only comes around whenever he hits it big; gambling in Atlantic City. Most people call him Big Tone. My dad's a real big man. He stands about 6'6" and easily weighs about 250 pounds. My mother has a small petite frame with curves in all the right places. She and I are about the same. We both have a smooth golden skin complexion and can easily be mistaken as Hispanic mammies. Some people say I get my vainness from her. She's a hair stylist at Suite 302 unisex hair salon. Her chair is right next to Ms. Toni's. Both of them can hook a head up!

I know all of my mom's friends – Rhythm, Jade, Starr and oh... I can't forget, Ms. Drama. Ms. Drama is not really her name. It's Sapphire. I call her that because she is the most over dramatic girlfriend my mom has. Aunt Jade and Starr live out of town, so we only see them around the holidays or spur of the moment events. All of them call me their niece and I call them, my Aunties. If I had to pick a favorite that would be hard; since all of them treat me like a Teen Diva. Move over Kyla Pratt, Ashanti and Nivea... Dymond is coming to take your throne, alright!

You don't know how many people have told me, I favor Ashanti. Personally, I think I look much better than she does. I'm not taking away from her looks because she's pretty, but um, I have better facial features: like my sparkling eyes that slant like Mary J. Blige's and my cute lips that are formed like the Diamond Princess herself, Miss Trina. I'm comfortable with Miss Trina calling herself the Diamond Princess, 'cause she's holding it down. If she weren't, I'd step to her. Feel me? It's possible, you don't. If you're not in the Hip-Hop/R&B world, you probably don't even know about her.

Anyway, I bet you already have the impression that I am conceited and I'm full of myself. It's okay, most people view me that way, but guess what? I'm not hardly sweetie. You are sadly mistaken. I had to learn early how to love and appreciate myself for who I am. Allow me to share with you a piece of my world.

Chapter 1

"Dymond! Get up out that bed and get your *bee-hind* in the shower!" my mom yelled.

I agreed with her that I needed a shower, because last night I slept 'ready roll' in the clothes that I wore the day before. We came in very late last night. It had to be past 1:00 in the morning when we arrived home. My Auntie Rhythm had a birthday barbeque. My mom was invited for the obvious. I was invited however, to keep my cousin Kera, (my Auntie Rhythm's daughter) company.

Kera and I are the same age. Difference is – she's a little fast. She thinks every boy that looks her way, wants her. She's always mad when boys ignore her flirtatious ways and direct their attention on the *'Queen Bee'* – me! At first I used to be all buttery when boys would try to talk to me, but I soon realized - it was all game. They didn't want me. They wanted whatever I was willing to give out for free.

Yes, please believe it. At 14, I'm still a virgin, and proud of it. Guess who's not though? You guessed it... Kera. Which she keeps as a secret from her mom, but brags about it to me all the time. She's always saying that I'm missing out on a good feeling and I'm like... *what good feeling*? I read and listen to all the information I need about sex. In fact, I talk openly with my mom about it because I know if anyone can help me, my mom will. It wouldn't matter if she was angry with me or not, when I need to talk serious business, she's always there. I love my mom. She may be hard on me, but I know she wants nothing but the best for me. Besides, when she's in a good mood, I can get anything I want out of her. (That was just a joke.)

Now, Auntie Rhythm, that's a different story. That's why I think Kera is off da' hook. Her mom has plenty of boyfriends. I don't mean guys dressed up in business suits, but the kind that look like, you know.... okay, I'll say it – Hustler's; whether they hustle drugs, bootleg CD's or movies, clothes or incense in the streets. I don't know, but they all have the same look – white T-shirts, jeans with Air Force Ones on their feet. All of them give her nice things – expensive things – mainly by well-known designers that I've never heard of. You might ask how I know. Well, Kera is always bragging about how much her mom's shirt cost. How much her mom's shoes cost, so on and so forth. I want to tell her, *'so what! .... who cares?'* ... but, I don't.

Face wise, I'm naturally cuter than Kera, but physically, she may be up on that one. My mom says she has childbearing hips and breast like a woman, that's how she knows Kera is sexually active. Even though she's hot with the boys, sometimes she acts like a tomboy. Her balance is a little off from being a true young lady. That does have me concerned. A lesbian might take her hardness the wrong way. Mom always preaches that females should be lady-like. She threw that in there when we had the discussion about homosexuality; which, I thought was awkward. The whole homo issue I think has gotten out of control.

"Dymond," my mom screamed again, "let's go!"

I was still lying on the couch. That was the first place my body rested when I hit the door. Yawning and stretching, I placed my legs onto the plush, navy carpet. I noticed the couch pillow was wet from my slobber. I turned it over so my mom wouldn't see it. She would kill me if she found out I slobbered on her new, baby blue sofa. It was bad enough that I had spilled barbeque sauce on my jeans. I was so tired that I didn't think about covering the couch with a sheet. I'm sure the dirt from my gear pressed into the fabric.

Last night, Kera had shared with me more secrets that my virgin ears couldn't believe. She and Manny (her new boyfriend, this week) went joy riding in a stolen car. When the joy of the ride was over, they made out in the backseat. First off, Manny is 16 years old, in Special Ed classes. Go figure -

him driving without a driver's license, breaking the law, with Miss Dum-Dum, trying to be that down chick – ride or die. Knowing if she got caught, she couldn't do a day in a Juvenile Detention Center. I can't front though... Manny is a sharpie. He's real cute. But, who wants a trophy piece in the place of an intellectual boyfriend? Too many girls in my school, that's who! The guys that are book smart - girls consider nerds; but the alternative boys, oh ...90% of the girl's flock to them.

When a girl dates an 'Alternative Boy', they get more attention; whether good or bad, from students. What is wrong with that picture? Why are most girls attracted to bad boys? I think it's because of the popularity. In school, it seems like all the bad kids are popular; especially, the loud mouth girls, the one's considered to be "the fighters", and we can't forget the basketball and football standouts.

Entering the bathroom, I heard the sound of the water hitting the shower curtain. My mother pulled the shower liner back, looking a mess in a bright yellow shower cap.

"Dymond," she called out, while lathering her body.

"Yes," I answered with much restlessness, trying to regain my energy. "I'm coming to get ready now, Mom... dang!"

She closed the blue tropical fish shower curtain back and kept on showering.

It was pointless to tell her that I'd rather sit home and watch television than to go to the boring library this Saturday. Had I mentioned to her that I had already pre-planned my day and it did not include going to the library, she would've given me that foolish unchanging straight face, as to say, *"You're going with me. I don't care what you had planned!"* So, I bit my tongue and waited for her to get out of the bathroom; still wondering why we always had to be the first ones to greet the librarians on Saturday mornings.

I pulled the shade up in my bedroom to appreciate the beautiful clouds, except - there weren't any. The sky was cloudless – nothing but blue. The bareness of the sky reminded me when Kera said Manny removed his shirt in the stolen car, to reveal his bare, rippled up six-pack. Why my mind wandered there?... I don't know.

My mom says that curiosity killed the cat. Though, my inquisitiveness was growing by the day. Maybe I did need to break my curious thoughts by going to the library. I wanted to grab a good book anyway; or maybe I would consider researching Lyndon B. Johnson, one of our previous presidents, for history class. I hated the fact that I picked his name in the drawing hat for my 4-page research paper. Nevertheless, I had to turn it in. It would account for 30% of my history grade for the marking period.

I was so caught up in my thinking that I hadn't noticed my mother standing in the doorway with nothing on but an oversized orange, terry cloth towel, staring at me.

"What's on your mind, young lady?"

"Oh, not much," I replied hesitantly.

"Are you sure? I can tell when something's bothering you."

What was she - a mind reader or something? I had something on my mind, but of all times I wasn't ready to discuss with her what I was contemplating. I'd been imagining lately what it was like to have a boyfriend. I don't know if she could understand the peer pressure, or for that matter, handle my openness. So, I lied to her. To the person I talk to about everything... my physical changes, emotional outbursts, my friends, my teacher's, sitcoms, books and even sex. I just couldn't come clean and say, "*Mom, I think I'm ready for a boyfriend.*" When we had the conversation before about boys, she told me I had to wait until I was 18 years old. Who was she kidding? She's from the old school. She better get with the times! By the age of 11, girls are already coupled up. I was well behind at 14 years old.

Anyway, I pondered (thought about) my eagerness, because Kera kept bragging to me all night about *Manny this and Manny that,* and how special he made her feel. She made me believe that I really was missing out on that feeling. Maybe I was, maybe I wasn't. Whatever the case was, my mom was looking directly at me with that stupid look, waiting for an answer.

"Mom, it's early in the morning. I'm tired, that's all. You had me out late last night and now you got me getting up to go to some library first thing this morning. Can't I take a pass? Just for this Saturday? *Pleeeaaase.*" I pleaded.

She began wiping her dripping legs with the towel. I admired them; praying that my legs would be half as beautiful, as hers. They are shaped to perfection.

"You never complained about going to the library any other Saturday, Miss Lady. What's so different about this one?"

Why didn't she leave me alone and let me sleep? I didn't want to be the victim of another lecture. Gosh! I wanted peace. Something, she wasn't giving me. In response to her question, I walked closer to her and reassured her again, "Mom I'm tired, that's all *okay*?"

Chapter 2

The library was quieter than usual for a Saturday. All of the employees at this location knew us by name. For the last past two years, my mom made it a ritual that included frequenting this place. Kera used to come with us, but stopped. She said this was definitely not the place for her; claiming it was too dead and didn't have enough action. So, instead of hanging out with me, she started hanging out with Porsha, Auntie Sapphire's (a.k.a. Ms. Drama) daughter. That's when I sensed things started to go downhill for her.

Porsha hardly ever stayed the night or attended functions that my mom or my Auntie's threw together when she was younger. She lived with her father, who had full custody of her. I overheard my mom in a conversation that Ms. Drama was declared a misfit parent by Family Court. She left Porsha in the house alone when she was 8 years old (without supervision) and went to work. From what my mom said, Porsha's father must have had a six-sense, because he went over to their house and found Porsha all alone in the house. She was crying and scared. Her dad immediately called the police and Child Protective Services. They removed her from the house that day. Ms. Drama lost custody and visitation. However, when Porsha moved with her dad, she changed. He was strict, enforcing rules she never had to oblige to. He had two other children by his wife that were older and younger than Porsha. Which meant Ms. Drama had cheated with a married man, - *mmm, mmm, scandalous*! Anyway, Porsha's step-mom wasn't the most likable person to live with. "*The Beast*" is what Porsha called her (and that was when she spoke highly of her). It was a proven fact, once Porsha became a teen; she did her own thing.

She rebelled against her father and *The Beast*. When she turned fourteen, back to her mother's house she went. Her father disregarded the court order and sent her back home. When Porsha's *bee-hind* touched base at her mom's, humph, all cat's and dog's broke loose! She got buck wild.

Kera and I attended the same High School. Porsha went to another High School, a predominately black Vo-Tech School that was an entirely different league. She dated Abdul, the star basketball player at Howard High. Abdul was three years her senior – 17, in the 12th grade. With his handsome, long athletic legs. Who? All the girls chased after him and he loved every bit of the attention. Porsha always stayed after school with him while the basketball team practiced. She would tell Kera about how many girls confronted her about Abdul. Kera, (all immature) would laugh at her, not knowing that Porsha was really hurting inside by that. They started rolling tough. That's when Abdul introduced Kera to his 'fun-dummy' brother, Manny. From that point on, Kera's mind was tainted.

I thumbed through an interesting book that caught my attention. Most of the older girls in school were talking about it. I wondered what all the hoop-la was about. It had to be a good book if it kept the 'Alternative boys *and* girls' attention. The cover of the book didn't pull me though. It had a big booty girl on it with three boys gaping, staring at the girl like they were, "*Blinded*." The author's name was KaShamba Williams. I thought that was a pretty name. It's sounded like a name from an African decent. Anyway, I had to put the book back because nosey Mrs. Ethan whispered to me that I had to be 16 years old before I could read it. I surely made a mental note to read it once I turned sixteen. I had grabbed another book. This time the author's name was Tracy Brown. The title was "*Black*." I lifted the book in the air for Mrs. Ethan's approval. She nodded, "*Yes*."

"About time," I mumbled. I wouldn't have time to read it because I had to get into my research paper, but it was coming home with me. I placed the other books I had out on the table back into the proper locations. That's when I seen him. Figuratively, I had died like Snow Black, waiting for a kiss from an African-American Prince. He was a brown-skin cutie with jet black eyes. My mouth was left hanging open and the books in my hand fell to the floor. I swear we both stared at each other for an eternity. I'm exaggerating, but that's how long it seemed. Maybe, it was only a few seconds, but it was direct eye contact. He couldn't have been an 'Alt Boy.' They rarely visited the library. He was at the library and here much too early to be one of them. At that moment, you would've thought I was in the circle of being inexperienced, the way I lost concentration, but I was used to the lame game. I heard it in school all day.

My mom was over in her glory, in the Urban Literature section. She loved those books. It was easy to understand her passion for reading, for I had inherited it from her. I love to read; and when I'm not reading - I'm creatively writing. One day, I hope to write a book and turn it into a theatrical play.

"Let me get those for you."

My eyes did not blink. They stayed on him. Was it my imagination or did he really sound like Ushcr with a deep southern twinge? And, did my ears deceive me? Was he trying to be a gentleman?

"Well?"

He wasn't even flinching.

"Sure," I responded, trying not to sound like an easy girl.

He bent down to pick up the books. His father taught him well; I smelled agreeable cologne. I quickly gathered my thoughts. I didn't want him to think I was dependant on a man. My mom preached too many times that a woman should be able to fend for herself. She later told me, it's best for women to have a plan – that plan, included a financial one. She would know; most of my Auntie's were independent, except for two of them – Auntie Rhythm and Ms. Drama. My mom says, "They will learn the hard way." I'm not sure what she meant by that, but I take it I will one day.

"So, what are you doing here?" I asked him.

He wasn't bothered by my bluntness. "Probably, the same reason you are here."

Oh, I thought, a gentleman, but a smart-aleck. "Well, you must enjoy reading then. What genre sparks your interest?"

Yeah, that did it for Mr. Smarty. He probably hadn't a clue what genre meant. Let's see if I can call his bluff.

"Genre, uh... uh," he stuttered.

He had to think about it; putting his hand on his chin, stroking it back and forth with his fingers. I knew I had him. While he was trying to play it off, I gave him the answer he was searching so hard for in his mind.

"Yes, genre. Meaning, do you like reading: drama, suspense, mystery, urban fiction, nonfiction, etc.? Genre is a fancy way of saying it, that's all."

"I knew that." He was obviously embarrassed.

So, he wasn't perfect. I had him all choked up. I didn't want to assassinate his character. I left it at that. My mom says, "*Black men are fragile. Black women have to hold them down, not tear them apart. They already have enough weight on their shoulders to carry.*"

"Well, answer the question. What do you like to read?"

He fumbled through the books that I dropped, handing me Rage Times Fury, by Trustice Gentles. I looked at the cover and turned the book over to read the attention-grabbing paragraph for readers to buy into it. It's called the synopsis of the book. Well, the synopsis was on point. It sounded like a good book.

"Have you read it yet?" I asked referring to the book.

"No," he admitted, "but I am."

"Good, how about we both read it and discuss it like the Read In Color Book Club? I can be the moderator like Angie Henderson."

He had a look of question. "Who's that?" he asked.

"Never mind," I shrugged. I guess boys weren't into reading groups the way girls were. If they were, he would have known about the sassy outspoken moderator of the online book club. Must admit though, I admired her business savvy (skills).

He started placing the books back on the shelf.

"What's the matter?" I asked him.

"Nothing. I've never had a girl approach me about reading a book together."

I smiled in a flirting way. "Guess I'll be your first... at least in that area."

What was I saying?? That comment threw him off guard. He didn't expect that. However, I was really questioning whether or not he was still a virgin – no need to be playin' in the Lion's Den. My mom always says, *"Birds of a feather flock together."* And since I'm not flocking that way, it's best I find out early if he is. Besides, I didn't know if I was strong enough if I 'so-happened' to get placed in that den.

"You never told me your name," he said directly avoiding my comment.

"Dymond," I said cocking my head to the side twirling my hair. "And what's your name?"

I was dying to know, but my mom says, "*Never ask a man first what's his name. You'll sound too desperate.*" Now that he opened the door to that line of questioning, I could ask - but only after he asked me first.

"Kyle."

"Well, about time Kyle. You had me waiting for ten minutes before you told me your name." I walked over to the teen section of the library to start on my research paper. Kyle followed. I held his interest.

"Why didn't you ask me then?" he whispered catching up parallel to me.

"Real young ladies aren't that pressed or aggressive."

When we reached the table Kyle pulled out my chair. Someone had surely taught him to be a gentleman.

"Thank you," I acknowledged, impressed.

My mother must have smelled the mating scent. Before, she was wrapped up in her book, now she was taking a seat at the same table that Kyle and I had gotten comfortable at.

"Baby, who's this young man?" she seethed through her teeth.

I knew I had to run down the drill in less than 60 seconds. If I didn't, I would suffer the consequences of a thousand questions.

"Mom, this is Kyle. Kyle, this is my mother, Ms. Melody."

They greeted each other by a handshake. I continued before my time was up.

"Mom, Kyle loves to read and seems to be quite fond of book reviews like me."

"More?" she bogusly smiled.

I had to think because we really hadn't discussed that much.

"Oh, this book right here," I showed her Black, by Tracy Brown. "We are both checking it out to have a discussion on it the next time we're at the library."

My mom must have made Kyle a little nervous. He was browsing through a book upside down and she noticed it.

"Kyle, are you okay?" she asked him tapping on his shoulder.

"Yes ma'am," he uttered softly.

My mom darted her eyes at me.

"Then why are you reading a book that's upside down?"

Kyle quickly turned the book around properly. He should've told her the truth that she was making him nervous, up there gawking in his face. I wanted to tell her to back up off him, but of course I didn't have the nerve.

"That's because I was showing it to Dymond." His slick comeback was whack. Even I had to admit that.

"I'm ready when you are," my mom said leaving the table unimpressed with Kyle. Any other time she wanted to stay at the library 'til the late hours of the afternoon, but today, of all days, she wanted to leave early.

"Alright, let me get my books checked out."

Kyle had a sad puppy dog look on his face like this would be the last time we had an encounter (saw each other).

"I guess that means you're leaving?"

"I'm afraid so, but we'll see each other again," I confirmed.

"Can I get your number to call you? Or do I have to wait until next Saturday?"

"Of course..." I toyed with him. "You'll have to wait and see me next Saturday. I don't give my digits out to every boy that seems interested."

He acted like he was disappointed. So what though! My mom taught me never be '*easy access*' when it comes to finding the right companion. In my case – boyfriend.

Chapter 3

Porsha, Kera and I were on a three-way call. I was enjoying the conversation. As usual, it was based around boys.

"So Dymond, Kera tells me that you met a boy at the library on Saturday," Porsha pried.

"What? Kera, why did you tell her that?" *Kera ran her mouth too much*, I thought. If I wanted Porsha to know, I would've told her myself. Dang!

"It's true, ain't it, Miss Dymond in the Rough?" Kera countered.

"Well," I said sarcastically. "If I wanted to tell her, I would have told her myself. That's so elle (elementary) of you."

"Pa-leeze, you must like him... humph, getting all uptight," Porsha grunted.

"And do!" Kera shouted. "She is feelin' him."

"What's his name?" Porsha asked.

"If you really need to know, his name is Kyle," I said right sternly. "And it's not even that type of party."

"Kyle Banks?" Porsha quizzed.

"I don't know his last name," I answered back. Who didn't Porsha know? God! For once I wanted to spit a boys name out and her not know whom I was talking about.

"Well, if it's the Kyle, I know, he's a new student at Howard High. He's a 9th grader on the varsity basketball team. And guess what else? His father, Kendall Banks, is the youngest principal that they have ever had in Howard's history." Porsha spilled out.

"Dang, Porsha... what's his momma's name? You know everything else," Kera joked.

"And do," I added.

That would explain his athletic legs. He was a ball player.

"Humph, all the cheerleaders are on him. You better know it... what you gon' do?" Porsha challenged.

"I'm not gonna do anything, but stay black and die, as my mom would say."

"There you go with that again. Don't nobody want to keep hearing about what Aunt Melody always saying," Kera hated.

I sniffed into the phone. "I think I smell – HATER-AID!" Porsha and I hollered out dissin' Kera together.

"Whatever!" Kera screamed back.

"It's a basketball game on Friday night. If Aunt Melody will let you go... I'm sure he's playing," Porsha hinted.

I wondered if I should take a rain check and just catch him at the library on Saturday, or go to check him out at the game.

"Are you going, Kera?" That would determine if I went because then, my crew would be all up in there.

"What do you think? Manny is going to be in the house routing Abdul on. Yes, I'll be there. You know I ride for him."

"But does he ride for you is the question with his ho-behaviors!" Porsha retorted.

I ignored Porsha when I should've stepped up to Kera's defense coming back at her with the same question about Abdul. "Okay. Let me ask my mom. How are we going to get there? Do you want me to ask her to take us?"

"NOOO," they yelled in unison.

"You know if we ask her, she'll want to stay; but if my mom takes us, she'll drop us off and pick us up after the game is over," Kera plotted.

"Yeah, that's what's up! Let Auntie Rhythm take us then," Porsha agreed.

"I'll still have to ask my mom about going," I informed them. I couldn't get around that.

"Not if you ask her if you can spend the night with me," Kera suggested.

"Then I would be being dishonest." *Lately, I had been pressured to do so.*

"*Exactly*!" Kera and Porsha sang.

Did I want to go through this to check out ole' boy? When I could see him at the library? But what if one of the cheerleaders was playing him too close? Would that mess up my chance? I wanted first dibs on him so, that made my final decision easier.

"Bet that! I'll ask her tonight," I chimed in.

"Okay, look Dymond, I'll investigate around school to find out more about Kyle. He's on the A-team and so am I; so it'll be easy to get information on him," Porsha spoke like she was a private investigator.

"Is he cute, Porsha?" Kera asked.

I hadn't given Kera the details when I spoke of him, but I wanted to make it perfectly clear – he was all of that!

"Yes indeed," I blurted out.

"Aaahh, Dymond got a boyfriend. She's about to get that cherry popped!" Porsha teased. "He's a keeper too, Kera!"

"Dymond! Get off that telephone and get that room cleaned. After that, come wash these dirty dishes!" My mom interrupted my phone time before I could snapback at Porsha.

"We know you have to go, but for real though... Aunt Melody needs to loosen up! She's too strict," Kera implied.

Instead of co-signing that check, I took up in defense of my mother.

"Maybe that's how your mom needs to be, 'cause you is off da' chain, Kera. Peace out! I'll see you in school tomorrow."

I hung up the phone thinking about Kyle, wondering what he was up to. I wondered if his mom and dad where strict like my mom. Did he have a girlfriend already? Was he a playa? Or, was he a 'real dude' type? These are all the questions that came to my mind as I began to straighten up my bedroom.

I cracked my bedroom door glancing at the black Barbie theme that I had since I was eleven years old and thought. I don't know if it was me, but I felt like it was time for my mom to buy me more of a grown-up comforter and curtain set. The Barbie stuff was becoming elle to me. It was time for me to pass it on to a lil' cousin, 5 – 12 years old.

"Hey mom," I called out to her coming down the steps while she sat lazily on the living room couch, watching the Ray Charles movie. "Can I get a new bedroom set? Barbie is um… kind of played out."

"Dymond, nothing is wrong with Barbie. You can never outgrow Barbie. She's like 50 years old," she said laughing at her own joke."

"Yes, it is mom. It's time to change it up," I mumbled hoping she heard me.

That was really my indirect way of telling her that I was changing, but I don't think she caught on to that. She was too caught up in the movie.

"You know what? Ray Charles was a mess," I heard her say. I wasn't paying her a bit of attention at this point.

I rubbed my feet on the navy blue Berber carpet until I reached the kitchen. I poured the dish detergent inside the sink, swishing my hands around in the water, creating bubbles. I placed the silverware in first and followed with the other dishes to get them all cleaned.

"Mom?" I bothered her again.

"What, Dymond? You see I'm watching television," she answered, agitated.

"Can I stay the night over Kera's, on Friday? I can catch the bus over to her house with her after school."

"Sure, if Rhythm says it's okay. Now would you let me be?"

Yeess! I danced in the kitchen brushing my shoulders off.

"Thanks mom."

She was either to intrigued by Jamie Foxx, or she didn't hear me because she never responded, "You're welcome," when I said thanks. I called Kera to let her know I could stay. She called Porsha and we both told her, "It's on!"

Chapter 4

"Dymond, today is the last day to turn in your research paper on Lyndon B. Johnson," Mr. Blossom, my history teacher, reiterated.

"I know Mr. Blossom, but I left my research paper at home. Can I bring it in tomorrow?" I begged, lying to him. I hadn't even begun that paper.

"No, I'm afraid not. Today is the last day. If it's not turned in by the end of the day you will receive a zero. Remember - this accounts for 30% of your semester grade. You can't afford another zero," he tapped his red pen on his grade-book. "Your grades haven't been so hot this marking period, young lady. If you expect to enroll in College Prep classes next year, you'll need to tighten it up."

My lips remained unparsed as I listened to the speech from Mr. Blossom with his stanky breath, always wearing the same dirty blue suit. I hated coming to his history class. We never learned about the African-American historians. We always had to learn about the European culture. I swear if he gives me a zero, I am going to form a revolution protesting this history class. "*Black Panthers till we die*," we'll scream with our fists held high! I'm not playing either.

"It will be in your box before the day is up." I told him. I'd put my foot in my mouth. I hadn't completed the paper, because I opted to read the book that Kyle and I were going to discuss. It was much more interesting than some Lyndon B. Johnson, alright.

I had a smart, (but a real cool) white girl classmate who always did her projects the week the assignment was given out. Her name was Shannon. I'm sure she had some footnotes about him somewhere. He was a popular person during report time. If she didn't, she could help me during study-hall time to gather some quick information and put together a few paragraphs – *something was better than nothing*. I had to turn something in.

I rushed out the class to search for her in the hallway. She was face deep in her locker shuffling around her papers.

"Shannon, hey girl," I said brown nosing her. "Your shirt is cute. Is that from Limited

Two?" She gave me that, "*What do you want this time look*?" I got straight to the point after that.

"Do you have any information on Lyndon B. Johnson? Mr. Blossom is stressing me about turning in my research paper and I didn't do it."

She pulled out her yellow history folder searching through all her completed papers. It must have been ten reports that she had completed. She was always on top of her game.

"Here, read over this and don't copy it word for word. If you do, I'll say you stole it from me!" she said, placing her brunette hair behind her ears.

"Thanks, I owe you!"

"You said that the last time. When are you going to finally pay up?" she wondered, shutting her locker door with stickers of Nick Cannon and Omarion plastered all over it. If I didn't need her report, I would have gotten smart with her, but I needed her, so I played it off.

"Girl, I got you! Stop buggin' okay? You know you're my girl."

I rushed to the computer room and copied her report verbatim – exactly, word for word. It didn't matter she hadn't turned it in before. My mom always says, "*Work smarter, not harder.*" Well, this was working smarter. Mr. Blossom would have his report and I would receive a letter grade instead of a zero. Holla back! One up for Dymond – alright!

Kera tapped on the computer room door waving for me to come out. I finished typing the last line of the paper and grabbed my bookbag and left out the room.

"What's up?"

"I need you to talk to Morgan for me and find out if Manny tried to push up on her?"

"Aren't you tired of going through this? You know he probably did!"

"Can you just do what I asked of you instead of trying to chastise me, cousin?" she stressed wanting me to feed her curiosity.

"I'll see her next period. I'll ask her then, okay?" *Here we go again, she had me involved with her twisted relationship a-gain,* I thought.

"Don't be asking her all scared either! Come straight out with it. If she bucks... you know what to do... drop her like it's hot!"

"Since you doing all this directing, you can ask her yourself, coward! After all, he's your boyfriend, not mine. I can lean back like Fat Joe, alright!"

"Be quiet! Just get with me after you talk to her... and for the record, like Lil' Scrappy, *'she don't want no problems with me!'* You can call me Scrappett, *cousin.*"

"That's what your mouth says. Remember actions speak louder than words and your actions ain't saying nothing, but your mouth is going a mile a minute. I'll holla at you later, *cousin,"* I mimicked her.

Entering the Communications Class, I stubbed my baby toe on the edge of the door and the pain hit instantly. I limped inside scanning the room to see if Morgan had made way into the class before I did. I pulled up my Roca Wear black denim jeans from the bottom and untied my butter soft Timberlands, checking to see if my toe was bruised badly. When taking off my sock, I wiggled my toes slowly, hoping no one was paying me any mind.

"When you gonna let me suck those?" Zachary asked. He was a natural pain in my (ask me no questions, I'll tell no lies) derriere. He flirted with every girl in the school and every girl found him annoying - even me. He was alright looking, but a pesky dude in and out the classroom.

"Never! Now sca-dattal, you idiot! Fall back and somebody might look at you twice!"

What better way to tell him to get out of my face with his fake mackin' ways? If he didn't try so hard, he probably could pull a girl or two, because he wasn't that bad looking; but one, he's nasty and two, he always has some ill comment to make about females. That definitely turns girls off... especially me. He was also a clown. No girl wants a guy that acts too silly... well, unless he had Comedian potential; other than that, who wants a jokester? Let's face it; his talent wasn't like that – he's no Lil' JJ.

"Come on, Dymond... wit' ya' cute lil' self."

"Zach, take a chill pill to calm your hormones, okay?"

My baby toe that I hit was red and had a burning sensation. While twirling my foot around at my ankle to get proper blood to circulate to my toes, Morgan came straggling in the class with her Mohawk ghetto-do pinned down tight to her head.

"Who want it wit' me?" she asked, tipping in like she was a celeb.

I thought, *'Sit your fake (ask me no questions, I'll tell no lies), bee-hind down and get a life, would ya!'* Since I very rarely said cusswords, you'll hear me frequently refer to that (ask me no questions, I'll tell no lies).

"Me, baby. Bring it on," Zach begged her.

I looked her up and down. We didn't have any qualms or beef – nothing like that, but I wouldn't go so far to say that we were friends.

"What's up, Dymond?" Morgan asked, sitting next to me.

"Life," I responded without much enthusiasm.

"You on that kick again?" she asked, smoothing the sides of her Mohawk to make sure her hair was in place.

"Shouldn't we all be? You are concerned with your life, right?"

"I guess," she stated sarcastically and turned her head to face the front of the class.

"What's up with you and Manny?" I said bluntly.

"We talk, why?" she asked, with her neck perched down to her shoulders at this point avoiding eye contact with me.

"You know why! That's my cousin's dude," I countered quickly.

She bent down to the floor to pick up her pen. Her pink dingy thong could be seen. Zach moved with her in motion to catch a glimpse of her butt.

"Dang, Morgan, is that all you?" he drooled, right childish. I didn't have anything against thongs, but I felt, for myself, I was too young to be wearing them. I mean what would I look like wearing a thong when my mother wears them? Get real; I'm not even trying to attract that kind of attention. Besides, thongs cut all up in your butt. I tried wearing them before around the house. They were not comfortable at all.

Morgan put the pen on the desk and grabbed a piece of paper preparing for class.

"Look Dymond, I'm not stepping on her toes. Manny told me they weren't together like that."

"Yes they are!" I interrupted. "He needs to stop lying!"

"Well, for the record, I'm not trippin' on that if he does still mess with her. He has enough money to go around. You know, so you can tell your cousin Morgan said... as long as the dollars roll – so am I. Case closed."

She was lucky Ms. Allen, the Communications Teacher, had walked inside the classroom. I was going to read her, alright!

I don't even know why Kera keeps messing with Manny. He doesn't mean her any good.

"We can carry on with this discussion after class, Morgan," I said letting her know it wasn't over.

"Whateva!" she said, agitating the heck out of me. "Who want it wit' me?" she repeated like she was Miss Bad- (ask me no questions, I'll tell no lies)!

Oooh, I wanted to say 'bee-aach', Kera do, but I held my vulgarity to myself.

Chapter 5

The bell rang and I left to tell Kera the news before she jumped on the bus to go home. The dull canary yellow painted hallway walls were bombarded with students, rushing to catch their respective buses. Outside where the long loud colored yellow buses were located, schoolmates chatted, (mostly gossiping about others) before boarding.

Posted up against the back wall near the bicycle rack, Kera was talking to Tan, one of her school friends.

"Did you talk to her?" she asked me blocking out whatever Tan was attempting to say.

"Yeah," I said, fixing my over the shoulder backpack.

"And, what did she say?" Kera lifted from the wall.

"Basically that Manny has enough money to spread for the both of you." I didn't go deep into details, because I knew that boys would down another girl to impress another one. I didn't want Kera to feel like crap, so I chose not to tell her about Manny's lie he told Morgan.

"There she goes, right there," I pointed.

Morgan was coming out the side door. She looked like a grown woman in her stiletto boots, swinging her long Mohawk weave.

"Let me check this girl," Kera said sourly, leading the way. Morgan didn't back down.

"It's about to be a what – *'Girl Fight'*!" Tan sang Brooke Valentine's R&B hit song. "*Kera 'bout to throw them bo-oows. We 'bout to swang them thangs!*"

"What's this about you messing with my man?" Kera said, removing her gold name earrings that Manny purchased for her.

"Well, Sweetie… I'm not even gon' trip off you, fighting over some boy! Manny confronted me, telling me that y'all wasn't like that. So, take that up with him."

"But the fact remains," Kera said, bullying her, "that you knew we were still boyfriend and girlfriend! How you gon' front on me like that? Huh? When you know how I get down!" Kera handed Tan her pocketbook ready to scrap (fight).

Morgan sucked her teeth. "Whatev-eer! Who want it wit' me?"

There she goes again, I thought. I hated when she said that. Kera yanked the long hairpiece hanging from her Mohawk hairdo and slammed her to the ground. Tan started stomping her in the face. I joined in, kicking her in the ribs while Kera diddy-bopped (punched) her all up in her grill (face).

People surrounded us, egging the fight on. One of the bus attendants peeled his way through the crowd to break up the fight. Me, Kera and Tan let up off of her.

Kera boarded her bus with Morgan's Mohawk weave piece in her hands.

"That'll teach her a-- not to disrespect me!" she said in between breaths. "Call me tonight, cousin," she said out the small squared bus window.

"I will." I boarded my designated bus to go home. I was so glad we didn't get pulled to the side; suspension notices would have been going home with us.

I dropped in the deep green leather bucket seat on the bus and placed my backpack to my side. My baby toe was already hurting and now, it was pounding after I helped Kera stomp Morgan. Everybody was 'big upping' (congratulating) me for the fight. Most of the girls couldn't stand ho – (ask me no questions, I'll tell no lies), Morgan.

I breathed in. After all, today was a good day. I bet Morgan won't be screaming, 'who want it wit' me?' tomorrow!

I threw my head back, closed my eyes and allowed my adrenaline to come down before the driver stopped at my final destination... home.

Chapter 6

My mom didn't get home until late. Tonight was senior citizen night. Instead of doing hair at the shop, she went to their apartments to accommodate them.

I went with her a few times. The seniors were real nice (most of them) I felt bad for some though, because they always seemed so lonely. Whenever I went with my mom, they'd light up, telling stories about their grandchildren;

though most of them hadn't seen them in months. If my Grandmom was still living, I would visit her, but she passed away from Emphysema the year I was born. It had to do with her smoking cigarettes all the time. I believe this is the reason why my mom holds tight to me. She didn't want to lose another loved one.

I had already talked to the crew and everything was a 'go' for Friday. Now, all I had to worry about was my gear (clothing). I'm not into the low-rise hip jeans. I mostly wear Baby Phat sweatsuits or I'll throw on a cute little tipsy-skirt or a cute jean, alright! I'm different than Porsha and Kera, as you've probably figured out by now. They only wear name brands. I could throw on a pair of no-name jeans and dress it up to look like Sean John was written all over them. It's all about creativity. For them - if it's not name brand - they won't wear it (like they can afford not too).

Both of them have Champagne taste with kool-aid money. It's worthless to voice this to them. They only emulate what they see – the current fashions and trends.

This was one of my restless, sleepless nights. In my bed I listened to the still of the night, staring out the window in the darkness trying to find the stars, the little dipper or something. Shoot, I'd even settle for counting sheep if it would help me get to sleep. I contemplated getting up to turn my computer on to play a few games, but I didn't feel like getting out of my warm bed to a cold unpadded metal computer desk chair, so I nixed that thought.

My mom stuck her head inside my room surprising me with a Nextel cell phone. She said I was deserving of it for being the wonderful daughter that I am. Gracefully, I accepted my gift thinking, 'I wonder if she found out about the fight I was in today or my scheme for Friday night would she have given this to me?'

I kissed and hugged my mom and put my new cellie on the charger.

"Yes!" I yelled tucking myself tight underneath the covers. That made me fall fast asleep with a big smile on my face.

Chapter 7

Mr. Blossom was monitoring my every move as I approached my seat in his classroom. Judging from the twitching of his eyelids and his lack of movement – in all likeliness – I was in BIG trouble! I was uninformed if I was, but apparently Shannon was put on notice by the color of her skin (bright red) when I looked at her. I tried giving her a signal to ask her what was up, but she kept avoiding me. Mr. Blossom called both of us to the front of the class. This teacher must have been sadly mistaken if he thought he was going to make an example out of me. I figured it had to do with that research paper on Lyndon B. Johnson that I copied off of her, but I wasn't going to let the rest of the class know that. Shannon's scared – (ask me no questions, I'll tell no lies), probably ratted me out like she said she would. There wasn't any proof that I cheated though. I had her originals.

Shannon's glasses traced around her pitied eyes. It was pointless to press the issue. As I neared the front, I turned to face everyone and kept walking right on out the class door with Mr. Blossom yelling, "Dymond! Get back in here!" But, who really cared? I was already in trouble for cheating and at risk of being suspended. What else could happen?

I shook my head walking through the bare hallways. Everyone was still in class – well, not everyone. Kera was cuttin' class with

Tan. They thought they were the only ones who knew about the blind spot (out of teacher's view) near the gym where people went to cut class.

"Dymond, what you doin' out of class?" Kera asked, as Tan tried to quickly discard of a cigarette.

I had to refrain from the low comment I was set to throw Tan's way. My concern was for Kera.

"Nah, cousin, the question is - what's up with that?" I said, pointing to the cigarette. "You smoke cigarettes now? You know how I am about that. My Grandmom died from smoking. Didn't you read the small print on the cigarette pack? It states cigarettes are hazardous to your health."

Tan stuffed the pack of Newports inside her pocketbook.

"Yeah, I hear you, but it's not even like that. I puff every now and then, but that's my thing. Now, like I said, what are you doing out of class, cousin?"

"Taking after your bad habits, I guess?" I said, sarcastically. "I'm only here for the class period. Y'all cuttin' all day?"

"I am," Tan proudly announced. What a dumb bird she was.

"What was the purpose of coming to school then?" I asked her. She seemed to find the question funny, but I didn't.

"Are you ready for tomorrow night?" Kera questioned, lifting off the steps. The class period was about to end.

"I'm ready. Have you decided what you're going to wear?"

"Girl! You know how I do!" she mouthed.

"Hoochie Mama style," I declared loud and clear.

Tan laughed with her stinking cigarette breath blowing my way.

"You never said why you were cutting class," Kera insisted upon an answer.

"Long story," I huffed. "Anyway, I'm on my way to my next class. Are you?"

"Yeah, I'm going. After all, this is the last class of the day. Meet me by my locker when class is out so we can talk and walk out together. I have a surprise for you," she smiled.

"A surprise? What is it?"

"Meet me at my locker at 2:15 and you'll see," she smiled again, but this time wickedly.

♦♦♦♦♦♦♦♦♦♦

When class was over, I did as Kera requested of me and met her at her locker. It was about four or five guys surrounding her, who didn't look familiar to me. The moment I stepped up, all eyes repositioned in my direction. "What's up?" I asked, confidentially searching them eye to eye.

Kera grabbed my hand. “Don’t worry about these doggie dogs. They’re always looking for fresh meat. They play on the same team as Manny.”

“What are they doing here?” I asked with curiosity.

“Come on,” she yanked my arm, “somebody wants to see you.”

“Who?”

“You’ll see,” she said with poise.

The entourage sniffed behind us with girls gawking like they never seen ball players before. They were cute ballplayers too, so I could understand why they were all up in our grills (faces).

When we neared the gym, it dawned on me that it was Kyle, who she wanted me to see. I looked over my clothes and asked Kera to check my teeth to make sure no food was lodged in between them. It’s nothing worse than to think you’re cute with food stuck all up in your teeth, in somebody's face. After that, I applied a gob of lip gloss to make my lips shiny. My mom always says, "*Before you go flexing and showing off, make sure your lips aren't chapped.*"

Manny and Kyle were on the court bouncing the ball, practicing their jumpshots.

My baby blue Baby Phat sweatsuit with my white Air Force Ones had me looking real cute.

"Uh huh, don't be posted up at our school! The game is tomorrow night at Howard, not here," I teased them.

Kyle grinned and for the first time, I noticed he had dimples. How could I have missed that facial feature? That made him look even better.

"If it isn't Miss Dymond In The Rough!" he stated, with his dimples pushing in on his face.

My face broke out in a flushing blush. "And is!" I replied, playing it smooth.

Kyle passed the ball to Manny and slightly pulled down his Houston Rockets NBA shorts to expose his boxers. He wiped his palms on his black headband and walked towards me.

"What's up, Dymond?" he asked, standing within arms reach, smelling all sweaty and a little musty.

"A shower for you!" I busted on him.

"Why you gotta dis' me like that? You see me out here working up a sweat."

"I was just kidding. Did you read the book that we agreed upon?"

"Yeah."

"No, you didn't. Stop playin' so much."

"Yes, I did. Do you need me to run the story down to you?"

"No, we can do that on Saturday. You're still coming, right?" I asked to re-confirm our scheduled date.

"Why would I miss it?"

Kera was over on the other side of the bleachers wrapped up in conversation with Manny.

"You never told me why y'all practicing in our gym."

"The floors are being waxed at our school and Coach Holland said it would be okay for us to practice here," he said with his eyes searching around our gym. "I think it's because he's trying to steal our plays, but whether he steals them or not, we are going to win. You know we gonna blow y'all out tomorrow night, right?"

"Yeah, right!" I said in support of our basketball team. "Coach Holland knows what he's doing, if your coach is stupid enough to let y'all practice on the competition's court, your team deserves to lose!"

"We'll see. Please believe, I'm going to dunk all on y'all... like this."

He was showing off, jumping off the bleaches to the court, gripping the ball that another player passed to him on cue dunking it, putting on a show for everyone to see.

"What do you think of that, Dy-mond?" he boasted.

"See if you can do that in the game. It's easy now. Nobody is on defense, Mr. Shaquille O'Neal," I laughed.

Conversing with Kyle, I had forgotten all about the time. I missed my bus! *Dang!!* I thought. How am I going to get home? I pulled out my new cellie and began dialing my mom's number, but was distracted when Kyle asked me if he could finally get my digits. This time, I told him yes. I could get away with him calling my cellie, but my home phone was a no-no. My mom had that on lock!

I excused myself for a second from him to ask Miss Hotsy how we were going to get home, since she was the one who recommended that we stop in the gym in the first place. She explained to me that Abdul (who missed practice) was coming to pick Manny and Kyle up and we could bum a ride off him.

See the type of stuff Kera gets me into! I could have easily called my mom, but I didn't. I wanted to spend more time with Kyle. He was beginning to be fun to hang out with. I was really starting to feel him as a possibility.

Chapter 8

The element of surprise is not a good thing. Abdul pulled up with Porsha in a white Ford Tempo. We call them buckets (old-style cars). It was a little tight in his ride. The backseat had bags filled with clothes and sneakers, making it literally impossible for four people to fit in comfortably. So, Kera sat on Manny's lap and I had to sit of Kyle's lap. I know you're thinking why didn't they just put the bags in the trunk of the car, right? Well, Abdul is alot negroidian and ghetto-fabulous! He had sub-woofers back there to boost the effect of his music. Simply put – he wanted that bangin' system and his system was in his trunk.

I could feel Kyle's breath on my neck, raising the hairs on my arms. If I hadn't known better, I'd of thought he was kissing it. The way his lips kept touching my skin. The moment was a little uneasy for me. Kyle whispered in my ear, "Are you comfortable?"

"Not at all," I whispered back.

Kera and Porsha had that matchmaking look about them ready to make a love connection for us if we wanted to or not.

"Kyle, you and my cuz a couple now?" Porsha asked. I shot her an evil look. "'Cause I need to know these things – to let your fan club know that you're off limits. If that's the case – ya' heard me!"

"And, will!" Kera added.

"No, we're not," I blurted out.

"Nobody's asking you, Dymond," Kera rang out as Abdul sang along with R. Kelly and JA Rule,

"If it wasn't for the money, cars, movie-stars, jewels and all the things I got, I wonder? Would you still want me?"

Porsha hit him on the leg. "Of course, I'd still want you!" she smiled.

"Would you still want me, Dymond?" Kyle asked, touching my neck with his lips again. What an idiotic question!

"How can I leave something I never had? Stop trippin'." My heart was skipping beats as I began to have a hot flash – which, I had occasionally. At first I thought only older women got them. Not true; my mother told me even young girls have that experience.

Instead of taking us directly home, we ended up at Mickey Dee's (McDonalds). Abdul was buying food for all us all. He didn't have to though; Kyle had his own money and was treating me, making Abdul put a few dollars back in his pocket.

The Mickey Dee's was located smack-dab in 'the hood' – centered in the PJ's (projects). This was Porsha's stompin' grounds, seeing as she lived only blocks away. Now, I told you before, I rarely visited Porsha – not that I had a problem where she lived 'cause we didn't quite live in Beverly Hills either – but because Porsha's mom is never home ... and we all know – *things happen when kids are left unattended. Don't we?*

I was always afraid that if I went there, I'd end up in a position that I wasn't ready to be in.

When we approached Porsha's house to drop her off, I'd hoped to see her mom's car, but as I suspected, the parking space that usually occupied her car, was empty. I sighed, placing a few fries in my mouth. Kyle was lovin' every minute of this.

Abdul and Porsha asked us to exit the car so we could go inside the crib (house). I was hesitant, voting against their decision, but Kyle, he was much too willing. He grabbed a hold of my hands, pulling me out the car, inside her house. Abdul had flicked on the big plasma screen TV with the remote control, flopping down on the red leather inch high couch. Porsha stood behind him watching as Manny and Kera crept off to the back room like this was already premeditated. The skin on my forehead rose up as I was feeling that this situation wasn't right. I knew my mom must have been looking for me. This was around the time that she expected me home. I had no idea that Kyle was this cool with Manny or Abdul to be hanging out with them like that. He didn't even seem like the type. I mean, they didn't appear to be his 'crew type'. Since his dad was a Principal and all, I expected him to be a straight-laced kind of dude, not thuggish. He sure fooled me at the library last Saturday.

Here I was questioning my behaviors, my integrity and most importantly – myself. My mom schooled me about these types of circumstances, but ultimately it was my decision on whether or not to take her advice. It was only five days after meeting Kyle, and I was in a house unsupervised with two other hotsy-totsys. Kyle and I started off with a great start – in the library. What happened to meeting him this Saturday to discuss the book? How did I let Kera and Porsha persuade me into going to the game tomorrow? Well, I really didn't see anything wrong with going to the game, but what about the way I exaggerated the truth to my mom? And, why did I allow them to make me miss my bus? If I hadn't missed it, I wouldn't have been put in this predicament!

Kyle's palms were all sweaty. Maybe he was nervous like I was. Porsha was massaging Abdul's shoulders.

"Dymond, you and Kyle can go upstairs in my room if you want to. My mom won't be home 'til 8:00 tonight and her man won't be back 'til tomorrow morning."

I couldn't believe my ears. No this hot-cock didn't put me on blast like that.

"I don't think so, I'm not you," I responded heated.

"I'm not saying y'all have to do something. All I'm suggesting is some privacy for you two, that's all!" she smacked her lips. Abdul flipped her overtop of the couch onto his lap. She giggled holding tight to him so she wouldn't fall.

"Yeah, that sounds like a good idea. Privacy – Porsha and me need that! You kids run off now," he said waving us off. *What was I to do?*

Chapter 9

Whew! I managed to escape my way out of trouble with my mom for coming home late from school. I told her I had detention for turning in my essay paper late. She understood that and praised me once again for taking responsibility for my actions.

I know, I know... you want to know what happened between Kyle and I, right? I know you do! Well, here goes... Seeing as though I'd never been faced with a delicate situation like that, I'm not sure if I handled it the proper way, but then again, *what is the 'proper' way?* What would you have done? Keep in mind Kyle is super fine. Chances like this only come once in a while... well, not really, but I'm sayin'.

Now, I'll tell you what I did, and then you can compare your thoughts to mine, alright. Kyle led me to Porsha's room, which was located on the 2nd floor of the house. It felt very weird at first – doing something like this. The shaky wood banister alerted everyone in the house that we were on our way to the bedroom. I couldn't look back because I was embarrassed to see the expressions on Abdul and Porsha's faces. Though, they were probably kissing each other and not even paying us any attention.

Porsha's bedroom door was slightly open. Kyle used his left foot, instead of his hands because he was still holding my hands tightly with his, to keep me from running back downstairs. With his size 11 Timberland boots, he jarred the door all the way open. The bed was made with fresh white sheets and a huge Tweety bird pillow. Kyle sat back on the bed and patted the bed for me to sit down next to him.

"Sit down, Dymond," he instructed. "I won't hurt you."

"And, I wouldn't let you. Besides, my mom taught me how to use my left and my right," I alerted him, punching in the air.

"You are so pretty. Even prettier than the day I met you." He tried to sweet talk me, feeling on my jet-black silky hair.

"Thanks for the compliment," I said pulling away – moving two spaces from him. As I scooted away, Kyle followed. I started feeling like he was trying to disrespect me. I'd known him less than a week and he was (because we were all alone in this bedroom) trying to get in my panties! When I looked at him, he smiled. His smile was too tempting. I was playing the hard role at first, but I felt myself getting warm with that tingling feeling my mom told me about. She said, *"If you ever feel that tingling feeling between your legs before you get married, RUN HOME! You are about to do something you have no business doing!"* However, I was too far to run home and I sorta liked this feeling.

Kyle put his long lanky arm around my shoulder, and reached in close with his face. He closed his eyes and I closed mine... and we kissed. I was inexperienced at it, but I could tell he wasn't. Maybe he'd practiced kissing with one of the cheerleaders in his fan club. I was thinking the whole time, 'my mom is going to kill me'! We french kissed for about ten minutes. He started touching all over my chest, up under my shirt. That made me really paranoid.

"Look Kyle, I'm not sure if you think I'm easy or what, but I'm from a different breed! My mom taught me better. I'm quite sure Manny and Abdul have bragged about how they've scored with Kera and Porsha but um, 'Miss Dymond in the Rough,' is trying to stay that way, alright. I'm not ready for this, so the best thing you can do is apologize to me for being so straight forward and hard up; and call it a day!" I said jumping up off the bed, leaning against the closet door, screamin' on him.

"Apologize? For what? All I was trying to do was give you a compliment, maybe a hug and a couple of kisses. I wasn't trying to go any further than you would let me," he said getting off the bed unnerved.

"Oh, yeah?" I said, getting back on the bed lifting my legs Indian style, holding tight to the Tweety bird pillow. "My bad then. I guess I overreacted."

I could tell he was disappointed. Who was he kiddin'? If I was selling – he was buying! But, I proved him wrong 'cause I wasn't selling a darn thang! Wrong girl – wrong world! He'd betta go check with his fan club to see what he could get for free!

My cellie rang with one of my favorite Ciara ringtone. *'If you're lookin' for the goodies, keep on lookin', 'cause they stay in the jar!'* It was my mom. I answered the call and told Kyle not to say a word. I told her, I was on my way home. It was perfect timing. She called at the right time.

"Let's go back to join the others downstairs," I suggested.

"Yeah, let's do that. Ain't nothing happenin' up here no way," he said dryly.

"Ok, let's go then…'cause, you're right… ain't nuthin' happenin' here," I confirmed.

"Are you still coming to my game?" he asked.

"Sure. Why? You don't want me to?" Now he was second guessing me.

"Nah, I was asking to see if I should invite somebody else."

"Oh, I see," I nodded a little angry. "Would that somebody be a cheerleader?"

"Why would I invite a cheerleader? They're always at the game," he latched onto the doorknob. "Why you buggin'? You're not my girl anyway!"

"No, I'm not, but I thought I was your friend."

"You are."

"Well, friends don't treat each other short (disrespectfully) when things don't go their way," I assured him.

That pretty much wrapped up my afternoon. When we got downstairs, Abdul and Porsha was rubbin' clothes! If we came downstairs a minute later, we may have seen their clothes on the floor.

Kyle and I went outside and sat on the steps waiting for the four-some to finish whatever it was that they were doing. After that, Kyle was clear (mentally and physically) where I stood. We had the best of conversation. He even told me he appreciated the fact that I respected myself, because so many other girls he befriended - didn't.

So, that answered my question... he was not a virgin. I was like, "Wow! What age is appropriate to have sex?" Most of my friends were only 13 and 14 and they'd already done it. I was fourteen and proud that I could still say that I was, alright. And, wasn't ashamed about it.

Chapter 10

Thank God it's Friday – (T.G.I.F.)! My overnight bag was packed and I was ready for the B-ball action. Why were the haters trying to rain on my parade though? Mr. Blossom had written up a slip for me to attend detention – ON A FRIDAY? – I'm afraid that wasn't happenin'! And miss out on my pre-planned activities with my girls – NOPE!

He gave me a letter that my mom had to sign. I wasn't worried about that either. I'd perfected my mom signature at the beginning of the year – alright! But, as far as the detention went, I'd have to serve double time for not showing up. It was cool; I'd knock that out early next week. I'd deal with serving the detention then.

Morgan didn't show up to Communications class again. She had missed two days of school. I guess that beat down hurt her – (ask me no questions, I'll tell no lies)! I was ready for her if she tried to bring the drama.

♦♦♦♦♦♦♦♦♦♦

The day went by without a hitch – with the exception that Zach was getting on everybody's nerves again. Kera was waiting for me at my locker (after pestering me in between classes all day about this game). You would have thought we were going to see Lebron James or A.I. (Allen Iverson) personally, not some high school ball players; although, Lebron is not the much older in age difference than we are. I think I heard on the Wendy Williams' Experience show that he had a baby! I bet that's acceptable in the public's eye, even with him not being married. You think it's because he's a millionaire? I guess if you have money, having a baby out of wedlock is okay??

'If you're lookin' for the goodies, keep on lookin' 'cause they stay in the jar,' my cellie sounded.

"Dymond In The Rough – speak to me!"

"What up Dymond?"

"What up Kyle? Shouldn't you be getting ready for the game?" I answered happy to receive his call.

"I'm in the locker room suiting up. I wanted to call you to apologize again for try'na play you."

"No sweat off my back. It's cool now that we're straight about how I am." Kera's eyes were planted on my lips watching each word form.

"Dang, Kera! Join the conversation would ya!"

"Don't get cute 'cause your lil' boyfriend is on the phone!" she said, frowning her face. "You know how we do. We don't hide a thing."

"What's up with her?" Kyle asked.

"Nothing, she's bipolar – which means, she has major mood swings – don't pay her no mind."

"I've gotta go. The coach is calling for the team. See you at the game and don't be cheering for your school. You have me out there to cheer for now."

"Whatever," I said, grinning ear to ear.

I reconnected my phone to the clip on the side of my jeans – courtesy of the Old Navy (good quality and cheap prices) and boarded the bus with Kera.

♦♦♦♦♦♦♦♦♦♦♦

Porsha met us in front of Kera's house. They lived on the outskirts of the city, but only minutes away from it. Auntie Rhythm owned a split-level house that was always immaculate. She was the Queen of house parties.

We stepped down into the living room onto the soft hunter green carpet and spotted the shadows of Auntie Rhythm and a guest. We couldn't see who it was, but we heard his voice – a voice that sounded too familiar to me.

"Daddy?" I called out with uncertainty.

Auntie Rhythm profiled, holding her glass of champagne with her long, gold painted, acrylic filled nails. Her cigarette was burning in the ashtray.

What was my dad doing over here poppin' champagne bottles, I thought.

"Hey Pumpkin, come give your dad a hug," he said with his hoarse voice.

"What you doing here?" I quizzed, at the same time giving Auntie Rhythm a questionable glance.

"Your mom taught you well – didn't she?" My dad said, laughing it off with Auntie Rhythm. "Melody, told me that you were going to be here. I wanted to drop this off to you," he said, handing me a wad of money. Atlantic City must have been good to him.

"Why didn't you just take the money to my mom?" I was quick with my response.

"Because, this money is for you. I gave your mother her cut, when I was over there. Is that okay with you princess?"

"Yeah, it's cool," I agreed. "Thanks, daddy," I said, kissing him on his cheek.

"That looks well over $500," Auntie Rhythm said with apparent envy. "I wish Kera's dad would come up out his pockets like that! He ain't nothin' but a dead-beat."

"Alright, daddy," I interjected before Auntie Rhythm got started on Kera's father, doggin' him in front of us once more. She made it known that he was a deadbeat dad.

"We're gonna get ready for the game. Auntie Rhythm, will you be ready in about twenty minutes?" I asked.

"Sure, baby," she said puffing on her cigarette, with that scheming look on her face. She better not try that shiesty stuff! I watch

Jerry Springer from time to time. I know how grimy women can be.

"Come on, Dymond. Let's get dressed. We're wasting time." Kera said leading the way ignoring her mother and my dad.

I was used to seeing my dad once a month. That was as often as it would get. Like I told you, he only came around when he hit big at the casinos.

Auntie Rhythm was wrong about the money amount. I counted $650. My pockets were fa-aatt (loaded with money)! I was only going to take a yard ($100) with me to the game. I knew I shouldn't have taken that much, but I was going to treat Kera and Porsha. I wasn't going to spend it all. I was going to save most of my money and ask my mom to put it into my savings account. The rest, I was hittin' the mall with.

When we came downstairs, my dad was still chitchatting with my auntie.

"I thought you were leav-ing, dad?" I emphasized my pronunciation when saying leaving.

"I told Rhythm I would drop you young ladies off."

"HUH?" all of us responded.

"Don't worry, I'm not staying. I'll just see that you girls get there safely. I got to make sure these young boys know my baby girl is off limits!"

"Uncle Tone, she already does that!"

"That's my Dymond in the Rough," he bragged. "Y'all ready?"

"Yes," I answered gravely. "My dad is up to something and I know it," I whispered in Porsha's ear as we walked outside.

"DANG, Uncle Tone! Don't hurt 'em with that pimped-out, red STS Caddy," Porsha said with dazzled eyes.

I suspected that my dad purchased his (new to us, but used) Cadillac Seville, symbolizing his winnings. Probably to reveal to everyone, he was still 'the man'.

Summarizing his behavior, I modestly acknowledged his ride. "This is nice dad. When did you get it?"

"I got Red Ruby two days ago. Check out those white-wall tires."

"Dad, that's not significant to us. Who cares about tires on a car? Maybe spinners, but not these kind of tires, okay?" I squelched up my forehead. "Can we roll now? We're pressed for time."

"Hop in," he said, gleaming like a boy my age eager to play a new X-box game.

♦♦♦♦♦♦♦♦♦

Daddy pulled up to the front entrance of the gymnasium and opened the car door for all us like he was our chauffeur. A few of the members from the Fundraising committee were impressed with his car, forgetting the fact they were out there to sell the remaining tickets to the game. We waved my dad off, but he quickly raised his brow when he looked at Kera.

"You might wanna pull your shirt down a little. I can see your bare skin," he confessed right fatherly.

"That's the style, Uncle Tone. All the girls our age dress like this," she played it off.

"Bye, Dad," I stated to him as he got into the car to leave.

Porsha had on a Roca Wear jean jumper with a belt looped around her hips. I had on a red Baby Phat sweatsuit with a pair of red and white Jordan's on. We looked like the young fly version of Destiny's Child, rolling up in the place.

The game was jammed packed. On each side of the bleachers, fans were squeezed in. A lot of people were there to rep (represent) Howard, but our school dominated in the stands.

Both teams were warming up. The cheerleaders were jumping around doing splits, cartwheels and yelling out cheers to hype the crowd up. At first, I didn't see Kyle, but Porsha's nosey bee-hind don't miss a beat. She pointed him out to me. He was near the bench lacing up his sneakers. Abdul was winking at every girl that shouted out his name, pissing Porsha off. Manny was seated one row behind Howard's team calling us, because he saved us some seats. And, guess who was seated not to far from us... Morgan! Only, she had her crew with her. We weren't even pressed. Kera stood up in her direction and shouted out, "Who want it wit' me?" and we all fell out laughing, calling Morgan out. We had a blast.

♦♦♦♦♦♦♦♦♦♦♦

The game was a close one. Even though our team exercised their skills, it was not what the doctor ordered. The prescription must have been filled for Howard, because they beat us like we stole something from them. Students from our school, Newark, were crying – like this was the championship game – and acting all petty, ready to fight. Kyle, Manny and Abdul were rubbing it in to everyone. We took the loss like champs though. All in all, we had mega-fun.

We waited until the gym was darn near empty to call for Auntie Rhythm to pick us up. Porsha recommended that we ride home with Abdul and his crew, but I said no – *this time*. It was already after 10 at night. Where were we going to go? Not this time! They weren't having me mixed up in that mess. I dialed my Auntie Rhythm, but Ms. Drama answered instead. She sounded a little distraught on the phone, but that was normal for her. I told you - she's a DRAMA QUEEN! While we waited for them to come, we kicked it with Kyle, Manny and Abdul. I noticed a few of the cheerleaders stayed behind as well, watching our interaction with them. I can say, Kyle wasn't paying them any attention, but Abdul kept glancing over to them suspiciously.

Ms. Drama and Auntie Rhythm arrived about 30 minutes after I placed the call to them. We could see them coming through the gym doors holding each other up. I tapped Porsha, who in turn, tapped Kera, which made Kyle, Manny and Abdul stop talking, to watch them. Ms. Drama was crying and her cries echoed throughout the gym.

"What's wrong with her?" Porsha asked embarrassed.

I wasn't sure if she was crying out my name, but it sure sounded like it. I think at this point, we all knew that whatever she was crying about – it was serious. We ran over to them and Ms. Drama grabbed me for dear life, screaming loudly, "Oooh, Dymond – Oooh, Dymond!" I started crying because I felt something terrible had happened. Kera and Porsha started crying too, asking, "What happened?" Ms. Drama wiped some of her tears and snot and sniffled up some air. "Melody was in a bad car accident and they don't know if she's going to make it!"

"Moooom", I went off! "Take me to her," I screamed, falling on the floor. Kyle ran over to help me up. That's all I remember... until Ms. Drama splashed water from the water fountain in the hallway by the gym, in my face. I remember opening my eyes wide twisting my head very fast trying to shake the water off of me.

"Dymond! Dymond!" Ms. Drama panicked even more while gripping my shoulders.

"I'm okay," I finally yelled, glancing over everyone that had their eyes pasted on me. I had never seen boys so scared. Kyle, Abdul, and Manny were speechless for once. Kera and Porsha were holding onto Auntie Rhythm.

"Well are we going to sit here all night," I thought to myself looking at them in question. My mind was set on going to the hospital to check on my mom. I felt real bad that I was faced with this dilemma. My mom's life could seriously be at risk and the last thing I can think of is – I lied to her. I prayed to God that she would be alright... I had to come clean (tell the truth) if she did. I couldn't let this remain on my conscious.

Auntie Rhythm startled Kyle with her words, "Kyle, you help get Dymond to the car. Now that she's okay, we need to be with Melody," she instructed him like he knew who Melody, my mom, was.

All of us proceeded to the parking lot with worried eyes not knowing what to expect. I figured since Kyle left with Abdul I would see him whenever. It didn't' matter at that point. My heart was skipping beats about my mom. I didn't know what to expect. What would happen to me if she were to die? That's all I kept thinking. My mom said to me before, "Dymond, always look at life with an optimistic view." *How optimistic could I be in this situation?* If I knew the full extent of her injuries then maybe I could visualize (picture) things differently, but from the expression on Ms. Drama and Auntie Rhythm's faces, it was bad.

Porsha and Kera were both leaning on my right and left shoulder inside the car as we sat together on the backseat. Ms. Drama started crying again, using her Kleenex to wipe away her tears. I put my head down and asked everyone to pray that my mom made it through. Someone had to be spiritual... I guess it had to be me since the adults hadn't recommended that we pray. My mom always says, "Prayer is the gateway to heaven. Always keep your line of communication open with the Lord. When all else fails, you can count on Him."

Chapter 11

I was snuggled with a Sponge Bob pillow in Kera's bedroom, lying next to her, thanking God that my mom was going to be okay. Didn't I tell you before that Ms. Drama had enough drama for all of us? Yes, my mom was in a bad car accident, but it was procedure to send a patient to the ICU (Intensive Care Unit) when they've had a head injury. They were holding her for observation to make sure she didn't have any internal bleeding. I don't know why Ms. Drama came to the game crying and screamin', "They don't know if she's going to make it." She should get an Oscar for that performance.

My mom was pretty banged up, but overall, she was alright. Especially since one of the first things she said to me was, "Ms. Dymond you are in big trouble. I received a call from Mr. Blossom. You have some serious explaining to do when I come home."

I was like, "Oh, my God!" After she said that, I knew thing were back to normal.

I tapped Kera on the back to see if she were still awake.

"Kera, are you up?"

"No," she replied.

"Yes, you are or you wouldn't be talking to me," I laughed at her.

"What Dymond, I'm tired. We had a long night."

"Do you think I should tell my mom about Kyle?"

"Are you out of your mind? You are already on her hit (bad) list for cheating and cutting class."

"You are so right. I'll keep that on tuck for now." I sank deeper into the bed. "Wait, before you go back to sleep, listen to my new ring tone I downloaded." I turned up the volume and sang along with Nivea...

'Feeling good, feeling great, look good, don't hate!'

Kera laughed and pulled the covers over her head.

"You won't be feeling great when Aunt Melody comes home. She's gonna dig all up in you!"

"Be quiet," I said hitting her with my pillow. She was right though, but what she didn't know... I was going to be responsible enough to deal with the consequences... *well, at least some of them.* Besides, I had a new friend that could help me sort my lies out – Kyle.

If want to know more, catch me on the flipside! Miss Dymond In The Rough is out, alright!

Please visit and join the youth group

at:

http://groups.yahoo.com/group/precioustymesyg/

Coming soon…

Book Two from the

Platinum Teen Series

"The 'AB'-solute Truth"

Reading Group Discussion Questions

Chapter 5

♦Did Morgan deserve what was coming to her? Why or why not? Explain your answer.

♦Did Dymond make the best decision confronting Morgan? Why or why not? What would you have done?

Chapter 6

♦Do you think Dymond should have accepted her new cell phone? Why or Why not?

♦If Ms. Melody knew about the incidents in school, do you think she would have purchased a cell phone for Dymond? Yes or No? Explain your answer.

Chapter 7

♦If you were asked to go to the gym like Dymond, and not know why, what would you have done in this situation?

♦Do you think it's wise to follow your friends blindly, without finding out their reason for where you are going? Why?

♦Should Dymond have called her mother to pick them up? Why or Why not?

Chapter 8

♦What do you think is going to happen next?
♦Would you have handled the situation differently? If so, how?
♦Who is at fault? Why or why not?
♦Were the girls really Dymond's friends?
♦Was Dymond being treated fair?

Power Words (from Webster's Dictionary)

1- Befriend - to act as a friend
2- Predicament - condition or state of a perplexing or trying situation
3-Literally - in a literal sense or manner:
4- Integrity - firm adherence to a code of especially moral or artistic values:
5-Persuad - to plead with: URGE
6- Immaculate - having no stains or blemish: clean
7- Wad - a roll of paper money
8- Acknowledge -generally recognized, accepted, or admitted
9- Ritual – of or relating to rites or a ritual:
10- Genre - a category of artistic, musical, or literary composition characterized by a particular style, form, or content
11- Contemplate - to view or consider with continued attention
12- Verbatim - in the exact words: word for word
13- Reiterate - to state or do over again or repeatedly sometimes with wearying effect
14- Scandalous - offensive to propriety or morality
15- Derriere – buttock
16- Moderator - one who presides over an assembly, meeting, or discussion
17- Dingy - dirty, discolored
18- Adrenaline - often used in nontechnical contexts - their adrenaline running high
19- Potential - existing in possibility: capable of development into actuality
20- Enthusiasm - strong excitement of feeling
21- Inquisitiveness - inclined to ask questions
22- Hesitate – pause
24- Gaping (gape) – stare(ing)
25- Entourage - one's attendants or associates
28-Consequence - a conclusion derived through logic
29- Investigate - to observe or study by close examination and systematic inquiry
30- Sarcastic - having the character of sarcasm
31- Revolution -a sudden, radical, or complete change
32- Strict - stringent in requirement or control